Alisha

SHIRLEY ROUSSEAU MURPHY grew up in California and graduated from the San Francisco Art Institute. She has been a professional painter, sculptor, and interior decorator, designing everything from breadboxes to beaded wedding gowns. She has written many books for young readers and is currently living with her husband in Georgia.

ELMO DOOLAN
and the Search for the
Golden Mouse

SHIRLEY ROUSSEAU MURPHY

Illustrated by Fritz Kredel

AN AVON CAMELOT BOOK

According to the Fry Readability Scale this book has a 5th grade reading level.

AVON BOOKS
A division of
The Hearst Corporation
959 Eighth Avenue
New York, New York 10019

First Camelot Printing, March, 1982.

The Viking Press, Inc. edition contains the following Library of Congress
Cataloging in Publication Data:

Fic   I. Mice-Stories
Trade 670-29237-0   VLB 670-29238-9

CAMELOT TRADEMARK REG. U.S. PAT. OFF. AND IN
OTHER COUNTRIES, MARCA REGISTRADA, HECHO EN
U.S.A.

Printed in the U.S.A.

DON   10 9 8 7 6 5 4 3 2 1

To Velma V. Varner

CONTENTS

ONLY

A LOWLY

MOUSE

The library basement was silent, dim. One tiny candle flame sent tall shadows stretching up the great bookshelves. In its flickering glow, the darkness under desks and chairs, the vague shapes of typewriters and filing cabinets, of stacks of papers and books, seemed filled with mystery.

Beside the candle lay an open book, and on the page sat a portly gray mouse wearing a flowered waistcoat. He read with silent concentration, his whiskers and tail still as still. Suddenly a tapping sound disturbed him, his whiskers twitched violently, and he peered into the shadows. "Elmo, stop that fiddling."

"But I'm only—," began a muffled voice. Elmo could not be seen. He was down inside a typewriter trying to find out how it worked.

"I can't hear myself think," Father said.

Elmo crawled out from inside the typewriter, jumped onto a chair, spun around three times, and leaped to the floor. Suddenly from above he heard the shuffle of boots. "Father!" he whispered and gazed with horror up the huge marble stairway which led past the basement ceiling to the library. Elmo was not allowed to go beyond the first step.

Father paid no attention.

"Father!" Elmo sprang to the table, blew out the candle, and shook Father's sleeve. "Father! The exterminators are coming!"

Elmo and Father dived off the table and dashed under desks and chairs, then in at their own front door in the wall behind the bookstacks. "Mother! Midge!" Father shouted. "Hurry, the exterminators are coming!"

Mother ran out from the kitchen flapping her apron up and down. "Midge! Midge! Where is that child?"

Little Midge ran out crying, "I can't find my doll!" Mother found the doll, wrapped Midge in a sweater, and the Doolans ran out their back door, through the mending and lettering rooms in the darkest part of the library base-ment, past great stacks of newspapers, and out a hole to the alley.

A gust of wind caught at them. They ran behind a trash can, found an old glove, and snuggled down on it. The wind howled. Through the library wall they could hear the tramp of the exterminators' boots. Elmo shuddered. Little Midge looked terrified. Father put his arm around her and held her close. Mother unwrapped the crackers and cheese she had hastily grabbed up and set them in the center of the glove.

From the shadows a sudden voice said, "Harrrrumph!"

The Doolans jumped up, ready to run.

"It's only Dimblehauser," Father said, settling back.

Out from the shadows stalked the cockroach. His antennae were thrust forward toward the cheese and crackers, and his beady eyes looked craftily at Father.

"Come sit down, then," Father said. "There is plenty for all."

Mother cut a slice of cheese for him. The cockroach took it without thanking her.

The shadow of a person flicked along the alley. A figure appeared, the wind whipping at her skirts. She paused a moment and seemed to look in to where the Doolans huddled. Then she went on.

"Who was that?" snapped the cockroach.

"Why, that was Miss Gurney," Father said. "She—" He was going to say, She often leaves her favorite books where she knows that I will find them. But he did not say it.

"Librarian!" barked Dimblehauser, flicking his antennae.

"Why, yes."

"Fap! Librarians!"

The Doolans looked startled.

"Librarians! Exterminators! Fap! *People! Fap!*" He puffed violently on his cigar. His antennae stood stiff with agitation.

Father patted his vest, took his gold toothpick from his pocket, and smiled affably at Dimblehauser. "Like death and taxes, Dimblehauser, the exterminators will ever be with us. There is nothing for a mouse—or a cockroach—to do but to pack off when they come and return home again when they are quite, quite gone away. But," continued Father, "exterminators and librarians are quite two different matters."

"People are people," said the cockroach. "They're all the same. They'll never change. That's the whole trouble with the world." He relit his cigar.

"But not all—," Elmo began.

"*All* of them," Dimblehauser rumbled.

The wind whipped into the alley sharp and cold. The Doolans snuggled closer together. The cockroach seemed to tighten his hard shell against the chill. "People," he continued, "are all the same—worthless, uncaring, and cruel. But then, I suppose, one can't help the way one is born." Dimblehauser tilted his head back and looked down his nose at Father.

People, thought Elmo, are *not* all the same. He thought of Miss Gurney moving softly to place her favorite books on the table for Father, thought of her smiling in anticipation of Father's delight. No, Elmo said to himself, people are not all the same, not any more than mice are.

As if reading his mind, Dimblehauser rumbled in his

blackest voice, "One cannot help being born human—or mouse, either, for that matter. One cannot help being born without a shell."

No one said a word. Dimblehauser rubbed his antennae together with vigor and smiled benevolently around. "One cannot help being born, ah, unfinished."

Father leaned back and held his gold toothpick up to catch the moonlight. "One would say," Father mused, "that a cockroach has a certain hard polish!" Dimblehauser, taking this as a compliment, beamed brightly. Father continued, "Perhaps a quality of, ah, of sharpness!" He seemed to Elmo to be relishing the word.

"While a mouse," Father continued, roguishly twisting a whisker, "is a mouse, is a mouse, is a mouse. Gray and same and lowly." Father sighed.

Dimblehauser looked uncertain and his antennae stood very still. Was he being laughed at? He glared hard at Father. "Precisely, Doolan. You've seen one mouse, you've seen 'em all. As gray and pudgy as dust-mice." He poked at a roll of dust which had fallen from the lip of the trash bin. "It must be very discouraging to be nothing but a mouse, my dear fellow, afraid to show your face in the daytime, slinking out of the walls after dark and then only to sit and read a book."

Elmo sat staring at Dimblehauser. Under his gray fur his cheeks were hot with anger.

UP THE
MARBLE
STAIRS

The next morning in the bright Doolan kitchen Elmo fiddled with his pancakes, pushed them around his plate, played with the scum on his cocoa, and finally, distraught and confused, blurted out, "Why did I have to be born a *mouse?*"

Father laid down his fork and stared at Elmo until Elmo became exceedingly uneasy. To avoid looking at Father he mashed his pancakes with his fork.

"You let old Dimblehauser get to you," Father said shortly.

Elmo nodded.

"I am proud to be a mouse," Father said. "There is no finer family, no bigger one, than rodents."

"What's rodents?" little Midge asked.

"Why, child, you are," said Mother. "My goodness, honey, haven't I taught you a thing?"

"Of course we're rodents," said Father, wondering privately what he *had* taught his children. "And no more interesting family exists. Why, rodents have traveled as extensively as man has, into all the far corners of the world."

Elmo gazed at Father, wondering.

"Eat your pancakes," Father said. "Old Dimblehauser is just full of hot air."

"And that cigar!" remarked Mother. "Smelly hot air."

"It's time you children learned a few things," Father said, pouring himself more cocoa. "It's time you found out who you are, and who your family is." He set the cocoa jug down. "Tonight we will go upstairs."

"Upstairs?" Elmo and Midge shouted. Little Midge's eyes grew big and round and she clutched her doll tighter.

"Upstairs," Father said. "And we will take a picnic." He rose and took himself off to his study where he could fume about Dimblehauser in private. "Sharp, all right," he muttered. "Sharp and cutting."

Late that evening they shut their front door and set out across the workroom and up the marble stairs. As they climbed the Doolans could see above them gigantic arched windows where moonlight poured through onto the towering bookstacks.

They stood close together in the immense, echoing Reading Room and gazed about them in awe. Moonlight caught at the vast forest of table and chair legs, shone with pale light on the crowded rows of bookshelves. It made the words and numbers on the spines of the books shine as if perhaps they were magical marks; and in the darker reaches of the library there seemed a kind of silent stirring, as of shadows moving there.

They joined paws. "Are there ghosts?" Midge said in a tiny voice.

"Perhaps," said Father, smiling. "Ghosts of ages past,

for here two hundred generations of men have left the sound of their voices, echoing down the centuries. And a smaller echo, but a true one, is the voice of mouse and his relatives—mouse the adventurer. Here are stowaways on the first ships that touched the New World. Here the rats who followed the Pied Piper of Hamelin. Here is the famous dormouse who sat at tea with Alice."

It seemed to Elmo as he gazed at the shelves that hazy faces peered from the books, that the shadows slipped away and beckoned him to follow.

The Doolans, still holding paws, made their way through the darkness under tables and chairs, past the huge fireplace, and beneath the arch to the Reference Room. Here, near Miss Gurney's desk, the encyclopedias stood in uniform rows. Father looked up at them, then moved deeper into the room. He stopped before a low shelf and put his paw on a single blue volume. "Yes, the *Larousse*," he said with excitement. "An encyclopedia just about animals."

They heaved and pushed and it took the strength of all four Doolans to get the volume down on the floor and opened. "Now, Elmo," Father said as he turned the pages, "let's see what you think about being a mouse."

For a moment Elmo just stared at the pictures. Then, "Wow! Are those *our* relatives? Wow!"

Mother stood on the page below the picture of crested rat. "He has stripes like a skunk! He looks like a skunk. Are you sure he's related to us?"

Father nodded.

"Dormouse! Dormouse!" squealed Midge. "Isn't he furry!"

"This says European mole rat can bore through the ground with his head, like a drill!" Elmo cried.

"Bamboo rat has orange teeth," said Mother with amazement, "and he is fourteen inches long." The Doolans lined up to see how long that would be, but as they didn't have a ruler they were only sure that bamboo rat was a pretty big fellow.

"Turn back a minute," Father said. "Yes, here are our cousins who can fly!"

"Fly!"

"Yes, it's flying squirrel. He's really gliding. See how he does it?" They did see—the pictures showed him in action. "Oh, my," Mother said, and gazed upward to think how it must feel to fly.

"Listen to this!" Elmo shouted. "Gundis has built-in combs on his hind feet."

"Where does it say?" cried Midge.

Elmo read, " 'The two inner toes of the hind feet have horny combs and stiff bristles that are used in combing the fur.' "

"That would save replacing a lot of combs," Mother remarked thoughtfully.

"Kangaroo rat can stand on his tail!" Elmo tried it, but his tail was too limp.

"Why, mice have traveled everywhere—there are countries I've never head of," Mother said. "How in the world would one manage to get across the ocean?"

"On ships, Momma." Midge remembered what Father had said earlier.

"Yes," said Father grinning, "stowaways. And not always did we cross the water; sometimes we stowed away in wagons and packs. Look here, black rat made his first emigration to Europe from Asia Minor with the crusaders."

"I bet we *have* been everywhere," said Elmo, reading the list of places. (There were plenty he'd never heard of, all right.) There were

America, Norway, Lapland, the Alps,
New Guinea, the Philippines,

Syria, Africa, Asia, Iraq,
The Arctic, the Pyrenees,

China, Arabia, Lofoten Isles,
And the Gulf of Bothnia.

Malaya, Siberia, Massif Central,
Egypt and Kamchatka,

Senegal, Somaliland, Europe, and Turkey,
Kenya and Tuscany,

And all of them settled,
All of them conquered,

By mouse and his progeny!

There were

>Wood Mice
>Deer Mice
>Jumping Mice and Voles,
>
>Birch Mice
>Pocket Mice
>And African Jerboas,
>
>Mole Rats
>Shrew Rats
>Sand Rats and Muskrats!
>
>Black Rats
>Bamboo Rats
>Old World and New Rats,
>
>Banana Mice
>Harvest Mice
>Cape and Spiny Dormice,
>
>*Norvegicus*
>*Amphibius*
>And *Mus musculus*—

"That's us!" exclaimed Father.

"What's us?" cried Midge.

"*Mus musculus!*"

"We're getting delirious!" said Mother. "I had no idea so many mice existed."

"What in the world," asked Elmo, "is *Mus musculus?*"

"It is us," repeated Father. "Listen: 'The house mouse (*Mus musculus*) is one of the oldest known species of domestic rodents. Its association with man may well go back to prehistoric times. Though charming enough, it is a formidable pest.'"

"Hmph!" said Mother.

They read of mice and rats who lived in trees, in waterless deserts and forests, and "In the water!" Elmo cried. "Look at him dive. I wonder how long he can hold his breath!" For the water vole was surely an underwater swimmer and lived in a nest hung on reeds.

"And snowy vole," said Father, turning the page, "lives in mountains ten thousand feet high."

"And look at that tail," exclaimed Mother, admiring the gerbil. "Why, whatever would one do with it all?"

The last picture was of zebra mouse. He had dot-and-dash stripes running from head to tail. "It doesn't tell much about him," Elmo said, "except that he lives nine thousand feet above sea level, in grassy places."

"Don't they tell what country?" said Midge, tracing her paw over the stripes.

"No," said Elmo. "Where else could we look, Father? Are there more books about us? How do you know who's a cousin and who's an uncle and, oh, *you* know! How do we get all sorted out?"

Father grinned and scratched his head. "One question

at a time. Yes, more books. Dozens, I should say, that include mice. And—"

Elmo squirmed with eagerness. "Can we come back, Father? Tomorrow night, can we come back and find where zebra mouse lives? Can we—"

"Yes," shouted Midge. "I want to hear a story about dormouse!"

"Can we?" Elmo repeated.

Father nodded. He couldn't get a word in.

SORE
THROAT,
INDEED!

They're going to be rough to get down," Elmo said the next night as the Doolans stood staring up at the rows of encyclopedias. "Do we have enough rope, Father?"

"I think so," Father said as he started to climb. Elmo followed him up until they looked down from a dizzying height. Father slung the rope around the shelf. They trussed up the METAL *to* MUSICAL volume of *Collier's Encyclopedia* and began to lower it over the side. "I don't think—," Elmo began, and looked down just in time to see his little sister run under the book and hold up her arms to catch it. The rope began to slip. "Look out!" Elmo yelled.

"Grab her!" Father shouted. Mother snatched her up by the tail and ran with her as the book came crashing down. Father looked pale, and his whiskers hung limp.

"I was only trying to help!" little Midge cried. "You hurt my tail, Momma." She held her tail tenderly and a big tear fell on it.

"We've got to have more rope," Father said. He set Midge between the stapler and the glue bottle on Miss Gurney's desk. "Sit still, little *Mus musculus,* until I come back for you."

"But I want to help too."

"You can help turn the pages as soon as we have the encyclopedias down."

"And keep your tail out of the stapler," Elmo advised and was off after Father.

Elmo and Father strung so many guy ropes and pull ropes and safety ropes that the bookstack looked like the rigging of a ship. "Library table, ahoy!" Father shouted. "Here she comes," and down spiraled *Britannica,* MAXIMUS *to* NAPLES volume.

"All clear to starboard," cried Elmo.

"Put more weight on it," yelled Father. Elmo had hold of the drag rope. Mother grabbed his heels just in time to keep him from being jerked into space.

"There's *mus—mus—mus—lus!*" Midge said later when she was allowed to turn the pages.

"*Musculus,*" said Mother. "Why, she looks a little like my cousin Laura!"

"Why do we have such hard names?" Elmo asked. "Why won't just plain house mouse do? Or deer mouse? Or whitefoot?"

"It's your scientific name," said Father.

"Are we scientific?"

"Well, yes, in a way. This name tells us what branch of the family we belong to. There's a regular guide to the classification of all living things. Our order, Rodentia, is divided into suborders, then superfamilies, families, and subfamilies, and then into genera and species. The members of each smaller group are more closely related. *Mus musculus* belongs to a subfamily that contains some 390 species."

"I'm not sure the children should be reading all this," Mother said with a worried frown. She whispered something in Father's ear.

"Oh, Momma, don't worry. The children are old enough; they know all about extermination."

"But it says we're pests, and—and that we make people sick! That we carry germs. Why—"

"I don't," said Midge. "I wash my paws every morning."

"Here," Elmo cried, "here it says house mouse originated in Central Europe."

"Wait a minute," said Father. He stepped onto the page of *The World Book Encyclopedia* and read, " '. . . in Asia, where scientists believe house mouse originated.' "

"They don't agree, Father!" This was something of a shock to Elmo, who was inclined to believe everything he saw written in a book.

"They certainly don't!" (It was a shock to Father, too.)

"Why, this says the word *mouse* comes from an ancient Asian word meaning thief!" Mother said. "I don't think— Oh, but look! Then it says we came to America on ships from Spain and France and England."

"Four hundred years ago!" Elmo said. "And we 'lived in the homes of ancient man'! *Are* we as ancient as man, Father?"

"It appears we might be."

Dimblehauser crouched in the dark between an unabridged dictionary and the wall and peered out at the Doolans with annoyance. Those mice are making themselves very important, he thought. That Doolan is putting some pretty grand ideas into the heads of those innocent children. I don't believe I've ever seen a mouse more above himself.

Mother stood on *Collier's* and frowned. "Why, this encyclopedia says we are low in intelligence!" she cried indignantly.

That's more like it, thought Dimblehauser. Let's not forget our place in the world.

"And that we have an unpleasant odor!" continued Mother. "*Oh, my!*"

Mice stink, said Dimblehauser to himself with satisfaction.

"And that— Oh, the nerve! Why, this is awful!" (It must be said that Mother was not making a very good adjustment to the encyclopedias.) "These people don't know what they're talking about! *My* songs are not involuntary! *And my throat is not sore when I sing them!*"

"Why, I never heard of such a thing," Father said. "What does it say?"

"That our songs are involuntary and caused by inflamed respiratory organs!"

"Inflamed—nonsense!" said Father. "I must say, someone is misinformed. You'd think that an encyclopedia like this would hire someone who knows what he's talking about to write its articles. Why, what are mouse children to think if they read this sort of thing? And that mistake about our origins. Someone should write about mice who *knows* about mice!"

Elmo was scuffing along the encyclopedia page with disappointment. "They don't have a thing about zebra mouse! There must be— *Father! What did you say?*"

"I said—why, I said, someone should write about mice who knows about them."

"Father! Why don't you!"

"*Me,* Elmo? Why, I—"

"Why not, Father? You could. We could help you; we could search through all of the books in the library for the adventures of mice, and you could put them in a wonderful book, a book for mice. A book about mice by a mouse!"

"Yes!" cried Midge. "Yes, Father, you write a book about mice. I would like your book the best."

"Why, I don't know. Why, it's never been done before. A book about mice by a mouse! Why, I believe— Why, Elmo, I believe that I will!"

ELMO'S

INVENTION

Elmo fitted a rope through a brass pulley and glanced up at the big clock in the basement workroom. "I'd better hurry. People will be coming to work," he said to himself.

He put a rope through the other pulley, then dashed across the room and under the door of Miss Gurney's closet.

When Father came into the workroom he saw a coat hanger sliding out from under the closet door all by itself. Father was startled. Then came Elmo's nose, and next the rest of him.

"Whatever are you doing?"

"Oh, boy," Elmo said. "I nearly got hung up on that darn hanger when I was getting it down. I got my foot caught right above the twisted part there."

Father watched him attach ropes to the hanger at either end. "Now," Elmo said, "I'm going to lay the hanger on the very top of the bookshelf and hook it over the back, so it's an anchor. Then—"

"Wait. Like an *anchor?*"

"Yes. Look, if you hook it over the back"—he used the top of a desk to demonstrate—"then these two ropes attached to it will hang down the front." He swung on the ropes to make his meaning clear.

"*I see!* Then what?"

"Then with the pulleys on the ends of the ropes, the platform will—"

"What platform?"

Elmo pulled a big piece of heavy cardboard from under a table. "The book platform!" It had a rope attached at each corner. "Look, a book will lie open on here." Elmo lay down on the platform to demonstrate. "Now if I tie the two right-hand ropes together like this, and the two left-hand ropes, then I can have just two ropes going from the platform to the pulleys." He slipped the two ropes through the pulleys. "Now we can raise and lower the platform to the book we want and tie the ropes to hold it in place. Then all we have to do is slip the book out onto—"

The workroom door was opening. "Shove it under the table, quick!" Elmo whispered. "They never dust under there."

They made it through their own front door just as the basement lights were turned on.

"Whew," Father said. "Say, where did you get the pulleys?"

"In the alley. The ropes, too. They were on some old matchstick shades."

"Does your mother know you were out there alone?"

Elmo shook his head. It had been pretty dark and scary all by himself in the alley.

Father poured more syrup on his pancakes. "Why, Mother, I don't believe we could have begun to search in all those books without Elmo's invention. When I woke up this morning and thought about trussing and hoisting and managing those great books, I just about gave up the idea. But now—why, now I believe that we can manage. And it's all on account of Elmo."

Elmo stuffed his mouth full of pancakes and blushed.

"I believe he's on his way to being a genius," Mother said. "Do you remember how he— Why, Midge, what's the matter, child?" Midge was crying all over her breakfast.

"I want to help too. Elmo gets to do everything! All you do is shove me out of the way and make me sit next to the glue bottle!"

Father picked her up and put her on his lap. "We're not ready to start work yet. We can't. And do you know why?"

Midge shook her head.

"Because something else needs to be done, something you could do better than any of us."

Midge gazed at him with tears running down her whiskers.

"We will need some white cards to make our bibliography and to take our notes on. You can cut them all to size so that they fit in a little box I will give you."

Midge beamed.

"It's going to be so exciting," Mother said. "I do hope there will be poetry about us, perhaps portraits. Somewhere there must be someone who understands about mouse singing. Why, we might even find mouse songs."

"I shouldn't wonder, my dear. Perhaps we will find the 'Song of the Golden Mouse' somewhere."

"The Golden Mouse!" Elmo and Midge cried together.

"Who is he, Father?"

"Where will we find him?"

"Tell us about him."

"You know, I hadn't thought about him in ages. When I was young, no bigger than Midge, my mother used to sing to me—let me see—yes." Father hummed a few notes, then he wiped the syrup off his whiskers and sang:

Through the murky treetops
    Witchy and creepy
Above the darkling waters
    Slithery, churning,

Races someone all a-shining—
Who can he be?
Follow the Golden Mouse, O,
Moonlight caught upon his coat
Follow the Golden Mouse, O,
Moonlight on his coat.

"I have asked others about him, and what place it is the song describes. Most think he is a mythical creature. But some say he is as real as we are."

"Father, will the book have chapters?" Elmo asked.

"Why, yes."

"Then could there be a chapter about Golden Mouse, if we can find out who he is?" Elmo was squirming with excitement.

"If we can," said Father. "But—"

"I'll find him, Father. If there's one clue to follow, I'll find him!"

A

BROKEN

ROPE

Where is Midge?" Mother cried. She had just set the picnic basket down by the fireplace and turned around to find Midge gone. (That is often the way with small children: they can vanish in a second.)

"I thought she was with you," Father said. "She—" He turned pale and dashed across the room so fast he was only a blur, and Elmo right behind him.

Midge was clinging to a toppling volume. Luckily it was on the bottom shelf. Mother reached her first. Father and Elmo grabbed the book. "Child," Mother said, lifting her down, "what in the world were you doing?"

"Nothing!" said little Midge defiantly (because she was scared). "It's the first book on the shelf. I was just trying to get started!"

Well, it was the first book all right; but as Father picked

her up and patted her he said, "We can't just look in all the books, honey. There are thousands."

"Well how do we begin, then?"

"There's a guide for us, which tells what's in the books. Why, it's all on catalogue cards, just like the ones you made, only people size."

"It tells about everything in the books?"

"Not everything. Just the main things. Then we have to search, too."

"Well, where is the guide?"

"We're standing beside it."

Midge looked up at the great oak card catalogue. It had rows and rows of small drawers, each with a brass handle.

They climbed up the catalogue and began to pull at the drawer marked MEW–MIT. It was stuck. Elmo clung to the handle and pushed against the catalogue with his feet. When the drawer flew open it nearly sent him across the room like a rocket. Elmo and Father pulled back the cards until they came to a card marked *Mice*.

"Why do the cards have numbers?" Midge asked.

"That shows where to find the books on the shelves." Elmo knew that much. "Every book has a number on its spine, and for each book, there are cards in the catalogue with the same number."

"How do you know?"

"I watched Miss Gurney put the numbers on the cards and the books."

"You shouldn't be looking out the door in the daytime," Mother said.

"But he's right," said Father. "For instance, for each book, Miss Gurney puts a subject on a card with the author's name, the title of the book, and the number. She files the card according to the subject in the card catalogue. Our subject is mice. Once you've transferred the number, author, and title of the book from this card to one of the white

cards Midge cut for us, then you can go right to the shelf and find the book."

Well, that was simple. "But what do the numbers mean, Father? Where did they come from?" Elmo asked.

"Someone named Dewey planned it all out a long time ago," Father said. "He figured out how to divide all the knowledge in the world into ten big general topics, just as Rodentia is divided into suborders. Only he gave his topics numbers. Then he divided each topic into smaller ones, and so on."

They copied all the information they wanted under *Mice*, but Elmo complained, "There weren't so many cards there."

"We'll go to *Rodents*," Father said.

"Father, could I look under *Golden?*"

Father nodded and Elmo raced away.

There were golden animals, all right—*Golden Hawks, Golden Hind, Golden Lynx, Golden Phoenix, Golden Swan.* But no Golden Mouse.

When Elmo hung his platform he discovered right off that a book pushed onto it made it leap away from the shelf with violence. "I'd better tie it," Elmo said, rubbing his bruised ankle.

Father came to help, and they slung a rope around the shelf and tied the platform snugly to it. Now the book slid out easily. They looked at the table of contents (there was no index), found "Rodents," turned to the chapter, and

Elmo began at once to copy. It was pretty slow work. "Father, how will we ever get this all down on these little cards?"

Father wasn't paying attention. He was scanning quickly through the pages, piling them one on top of the other over Elmo as he diligently copied away.

"Look at this!" Father cried. "We know we traveled in ships, and it says here perhaps in native canoes to the islands of Oceania. But listen! There were rats on the Galápagos Islands *before* man! This book says they must have drifted there alone on natural rafts. That's a trip of five hundred miles! When man came they had already developed their own distinct species."

That made Elmo pretty proud of what a rodent could do when he set his mind to it. But still there was the problem of the notes. "Father, why do my notes take so much longer than yours do? Yours are shorter. How do you do that?"

"I don't put down every word. Just the necessary ones. Look, you make an outline. Very brief, main topic first, then those things that belong to it indented underneath."

Elmo tried. He tried again. Finally he thought he had it.

STRIPED TREE MOUSE:
    Lives in open birch woods
    Eats seeds
    In cold climates sleeps:
        All winter
        In hollow tree

"That's it!" Father said. "Remember to put only one subject on a card, and to note author, title, and number on each card. That way we can separate the cards later by subject and know where to locate the books. You're going to make a good researcher, Elmo."

As the Doolans took notes, Dimblehauser moved silently behind the books at the back of the shelf, paused in the shadows, and peered out at them. *Those mice are not just putting on airs, they are utterly mad! Who ever heard of mice doing research! They need a little comeuppance.* He settled himself comfortably beside the rope which Elmo had tied around the shelf. It was nice and dark back there, nice and warm, and the rope tasted very good. Dimblehauser chewed with contentment.

"This is all very well," Mother was saying, "but it's facts and more facts, and not one thing about poetry or song! I know I shouldn't be impatient, but . . ."

"Why, we only just began in the catalogue," Father said. "We've done the specific things, *Mice* and then *Rodents,* but we haven't yet looked for the more general things, Mother—*Animals in art, in literature,* and *in mythology.*" He paused to help pull out the next book.

"In mythology, Father? Would Golden Mouse be there, if he was a myth?" Elmo asked.

The platform wiggled a little, but they all knew it was tied. "He might be," Father said, "if—" The book hit the platform, the platform leaped away from the shelf, and the

Doolans flew in four different directions. Elmo tried to grab a rope and missed. The book hit the floor with a *bang!* Elmo landed beside it with a dull thud. He lay very still.

Mother clung to a shelf, Father hung from the platform by one paw, and little Midge dangled by the belt of her dress from Father's weakening grasp. With effort he pulled her up and set her on the platform, then climbed down to stare with consternation at the still form of his son. "Elmo, say something."

Elmo opened his eyes and said, "Uff."

Mother rubbed Elmo's wrists and looked worried. Little Midge put her arms around him. Father, when he found Elmo had no broken bones, climbed up to examine the rope. "That was a good strong rope," he said. "I wonder how that happened."

Elmo wondered too. That rope did not look broken, it looked—"Chewed!" Elmo said. Father looked at Elmo. Elmo looked at Father. They were both thinking the same thing.

As Father built a mouse-sized fire in the huge fireplace and Mother laid out their supper of little meat pies, cheese custard, and hot and fragrant cocoa, Elmo sat sorting Mother's cards for her, putting them in order by number. She had been back to the catalogue and had got so excited over what she found there that her poor children had to call her three times to come down for supper. "I *did not* find a subject heading for *Animals in mythology*," Mother said accusingly, looking straight at Father. "I had to look under *Mythology*, and that drawer was stuck terribly!"

Father grinned. "Never a dull moment, Momma. The exercise is good for the figure."

As he sorted, Elmo quietly copied some of Mother's cards and slipped them into his pocket. He thought he might do a little sleuthing on his own for a clue to Golden Mouse.

FIVE

GOLDEN

MICE

Elmo slipped out his front door early Sunday morning with a Roquefort cheese-pickle-and-syrup sandwich and his cards. As he climbed the stairs, the library seemed to Elmo even larger and more silent than it did at night.

He found the book he wanted and had a time getting it out. Once he lost control and it nearly fell on him. (It was Funk and Wagnall's *Standard Dictionary of Folklore, Mythology, and Legend,* volume two, and just as heavy as it sounds.)

When he got to "Mouse," the first thing he read was, "It is reported that mice were created . . . by the Devil." That was a lively beginning, and it went right on to give other ways in which mice were created, such as: they fall to earth from storm clouds; witches make mice (in Germany they are brewed in a pot of herbs); and mice come from little balls of earth thrown over a human shoulder. He moved down the page, then—"Wow!" he shouted. His voice may have been small, but it echoed loudly among the bookstacks. "Wow, I've found him! Yippee!" He jumped up and down on the page right where it said "five golden mice." "Oh, boy!" Elmo yelled, and when he had calmed down sufficiently he read, "Mice as ministers of vengeance plagued the Philistines who had taken the Ark of God from the camp of the Israelites. They returned it later with five golden mice."

It was not clear to Elmo who the Philistines were, or the Israelites either, for that matter. But it was perfectly clear that he had found a terrific clue to Golden Mouse. He read on down the page hoping to find out more. He didn't, but his notes showed that:

People's souls emerge from their bodies:

> In form of mice
> At times of:
>> Sleep
>> Death

Mice:

> Flee from a house when there is a death
>> [Could this be the soul? Elmo wondered.]
> Cause forgetfulness in Jewish people by nibbling
>> their food

Foretell war by appearing in great numbers
Rats:
Desert a sinking ship

When he got down the page to "fried mice and mouse-pie" Elmo felt a little uncomfortable. But he read it anyway. It seemed that fried mice and mouse-pie were used as cures for bed-wetting. Cooked mice were also recommended for smallpox, whooping cough, and measles, and mouse ashes mixed with honey for earaches and bad breath. Elmo read every word, but he wished afterward he hadn't. It gave him nightmares. When he told Father, Father said he was sorry; then he said, "That's research, Elmo. A mouse can't afford to be squeamish."

Elmo got pretty edgy taking notes on "The Mouse Tower," a story about a heartless miser being eaten alive by mice or rats. The story was complicated; he tore up seven cards before he had it down right, but he was determined to get such an unusual story. When he thought he had it all down, there at the bottom was *See* HATTO, and that was in volume one.

This volume isn't going to fall on me, Elmo thought to himself. He slung a rope around it and pushed it out from behind.

There were a good many versions of the story under HATTO, but Elmo was stubborn and he stayed with it. He climbed down weak from hunger and mental exertion and took his Roquefort cheese-pickle-and-syrup sandwich to the top of Miss Gurney's desk. He leaned against a box of paper clips and thought about the five golden mice and wondered what the rest of the story was. When he finished half his sandwich, he put his paws behind his head and leaned back.

"Why, I've never seen that before!" Elmo said. "I wonder if it's always been there." It was a huge machine standing on a table next to Miss Gurney's desk. It had a great cave in its middle. The cave floor, even with the desk top, was smooth, white, and tilted. It made a terrific slide.

At the very top were some knobs and two round glass plates. On the side nearest Miss Gurney's desk was a switch. By climbing on Miss Gurney's stack of unanswered letters he could reach it. It made a light go on inside the cave. Elmo was just considering what this might be for when he became aware that someone was watching him. Oh, boy, he thought. I don't want to be caught up here fiddling with this machine, and with my Roquefort cheese-pickle-and-syrup sandwich all over Miss Gurney's desk. He was ready to run when he caught sight of the culprit. "What are you doing up here?" Elmo asked.

"I followed you." Little Midge came out from the shadows. "I've been watching you all morning, and now I'm hungry!"

Elmo gave her the other half of his sandwich.

"Did you really find Golden Mouse?" Midge whispered.

"Yes. And now we're going to look in *The Golden Bough*, and we might find more there."

It was twice as hard to get the first volume out with Midge helping. Elmo sure didn't want to smash his little sister.

"Here's something different," Elmo said. "Mice are always accused of stealing from people, but here are *people* stealing from *mice*."

"Where? Read it."

"The people of Kamchatka"—Father said later that was in Russia—" 'rob the field mice of the bulbs which these little creatures have laid up in their burrows as a store against winter.' "

"How mean!"

"Then they leave old rags and broken needles in return. What does that make you think of, Midge?"

"I know! Pack rats! They collect bits of glass and pocket watches and paring knives from people and leave pebbles in return."

Elmo grinned. "Think how it would be if the people of Kamchatka and the pack rats ever got together. Back and forth, back and forth, why, they might never be done trading."

Later they found that human children lose their teeth just as mice do. This delighted Midge. "Did you know human children put their teeth in mouse holes?" she said. She made a poem for them:

> Put your tooth in a mouse's home,
> The new will grow as hard as stone.

"Here, this puts dormouse in Paris in 1874," Elmo said. "But— *Oh, drat!*"

"What's the matter?"

"They were *not* golden mice I found, not *real* ones!"

"What, then?"

"Metal gold. Images of mice. Oh, double drat!"

"But Elmo, real gold, like money? That's something." Elmo didn't care. He was furious.

"Does it *say* these are the same ones you found in the other book?"

Elmo read it again. "Well not exactly. It says, 'The Philistines made golden images of the vermin'—that's us— 'and sent them out of the country in a new cart drawn by two cows, hoping that the real mice would simultaneously depart.' It gives a funny reference." Elmo copied it down. "What are you crying about?"

"Because people steal from us, and call us vermin, and try to drive us away! Maybe old Dim—Mr. Dimble-hauser was right! Maybe people . . ."

"Don't be silly," Elmo said gruffly. "Why, look here, right under your tail. It says, 'Four pairs of mice are sol-emnly united in marriage by the priest.' Think of that.

Married by a human priest. And then—and then— Come on, Midge, let's go look at that machine."

"What does it say? Tell me the rest!"

"Oh, bother. It says each pair is shut in a canoe with some rice and escorted to the seashore just like in a real wedding. As the procession passes, the people beat on rice blocks. Then the canoes are launched and 'left to the mercy of the winds and waves.' Well, you wanted to hear it!"

Elmo showed Midge the machine and how to slide down the cave floor, and that cheered her. He climbed up to turn on the light, then climbed all over it to investigate. He wiggled all the knobs and then stuck his head in between the glass plate and the light to see if he could see down inside the machine.

"Yow!" Midge yelled. When Elmo looked down she was clear across the room, cowering under a chair. "There's a giant in that machine!"

"A giant what?"

"A giant rat! A huge one!"

Elmo climbed down to look, but there was nothing. It took a long time to get Midge out from under the chair, and that gave Elmo time to think.

Finally, Midge let herself be boosted up on top of the machine.

"Now," Elmo said, "put your head under the glass, but don't look at the light, it's too bright." He leaped down and into the cave.

"It's warm," Midge called with surprise when she had her head under.

"Wow!" Elmo nearly ran under the chair too. The shadow of a giant mouse head covered the floor of the machine. Its whiskers alone were twice as long as Elmo. "Wiggle your whiskers," Elmo said.

Midge did. So did the creature.

"Twitch your nose."

She twitched. So did it.

"Well," Elmo said later as he was trying to puzzle it out, "that machine sure wasn't built to magnify mice! But it was built to magnify something, and I'd like to find out what."

A REAL

CLUE

That night Elmo and Father stood on the open Bible and read, in Samuel, how God had wrought vengeance upon the Philistines for stealing the Ark of God, and how "A deadly panic raged throughout the entire city; the hand of God was very heavy there," and how the golden mice were guilt offerings made by the Philistines, along with plague-boils made of gold.

"Plague-boils! Ugh!" Elmo said. "Well, at least I have one clue to who the real Golden Mouse might be, because some New World mice live in forests and swamps, and that sounds like the place in the song. But it isn't much," Elmo added. "There *is* a golden hamster, Father! But he lives underground, so I guess he doesn't go about in trees so much."

"Father! Elmo!" Midge raced around the edge of the stack, skidded, got her feet tangled in her tail, and tumbled and slid on the slick floor. She bounced up quick as a wink.

"Come see what we've found! Come *see!*"

"Child, you gave me a turn. What did you find?"

"Come and see!"

"Is it Golden Mouse?" Elmo cried.

"No. It's ivory!"

Elmo and Father followed Midge to the 800s and up to Mother's high-slung platform. (There were three platforms now. Elmo had been back to the alley.)

Mother was sitting on the margin, gazing in rapture at the picture of a beautiful rat carved out of ivory. His lifelike tail was curled around his body, the tip of it held in his delicate paw. He had a gentle face and great, tender eyes, and he was looking up as if in adoration. His ears were small and smooth as any mouse's ears.

He was *nezumi,* which means "rat" in Japanese.

They made themselves comfortable where they could admire the picture, and Mother told them the story.

"In Japan, the rat is one of the twelve animals who marks the months of the year. Each animal stands for a month, but the cat stands for none. He is not included, and this is why:

"When the great Buddha was dying, a young rat, faint with hunger after a long and exhausting journey to pay his last respects, stopped by the altar to lick up a bit of wax from one of the candles. The cat, seeing him, pounced on him and ate him.

"For this transgression against the law of Buddha, the cat was excluded forever from the honored place in the zodiac, and the rat was included among the twelve privileged animals."

In the same book they found their second hero, a white rat. At one time the people of Japan favored Daikoku, god of wealth and prosperity, over all other Buddhist gods. Those gods grew angry at this and asked Emma-o, King of Hell, to get rid of Daikoku.

Emma-o sent the demon, Shiro, to earth, and guided by a sparrow, Shiro searched for Daikoku. But Daikoku, hearing footsteps, sent his chief rat to see who was coming. When the rat discovered Shiro he ran into the garden, plucked a twig from the sacred tree, and chased the demon clear through the gate of Hell, and Daikoku was saved.

Mother began to make a little drawing of *nezumi*.

It was much later, when the moon had sunk low and Elmo was thinking fondly of midnight supper, that he found the clue. "I knew I'd find it tonight! I knew it! Father!" Elmo was jumping up and down on the index.

Father was so engrossed in what he was doing he didn't even hear.

"Father!" Elmo screamed. His heart beat so fast he could hardly turn the pages.

The index read, "Mouse, deer, 129, 211; Golden, 127, 129."

"Father! I've found Golden Mouse!"

Father heard him that time. He came running.

Elmo fumbled with the pages. What if it was a false

alarm? There, page 127. He couldn't bear to be disappointed again. Father landed with a thud beside him. "Where?"

They read it together: "Land of the Golden Mouse, land of the unstable earth, the great Okefenokee Swamp spread away under the heat of the spring sun." But then there was no more about Golden Mouse. Not on that page, not on the next. Alligators, black-shelled turtles as big as dishpans, but no Golden Mouse.

"Still," Elmo said, "it's telling us what it's like where he lives. It's telling us he's real! *Father, he's real! I found Golden Mouse and he's real!*"

Father backed to the edge of the book, rubbed his ear, and grinned.

"The Okefenokee Swamp!" Elmo yelled, and did a handspring over the word *Okefenokee*. "Wow!"

"Hmmm," Father said, twisting a whisker. "Move off *Okefenokee*, Elmo. Look here."

Together they read: " . . . the vast shallow bog of the Okefenokee—once a depression in a prehistoric sea—was extending its 400,000 acres in an immense caldron of life."

But there was no more about Golden Mouse himself. Until—there, on page 129! Elmo read, " 'A foot or so above the ground, in a clump of weeds, we saw' "— Elmo was so excited he was shouting it all—" 'the home of the Golden Mouse.' " He was in such a dither he was chewing on the end of his tail. When he tried to write he found he was holding his tail instead of the pencil.

" '. . . thick, soft, reddish-gold fur.' " Elmo jumped up and down. "He's *real!*"

Together they read how Golden Mouse could cross a swamp canal by swimming under water and come out the other side as dry as a duck, how he often built his nest in an abandoned bird's nest, making a dome over the top to keep it warm and dry. And then—then there really was no more about Golden Mouse, but they did learn that the Okefenokee Swamp is on the border between Florida and Georgia.

"He's a southern mouse then," Father said.

Elmo tumbled into bed that night, thinking, "Now that I know where he lives, I can find all about Golden Mouse. I just have to look up Okefenokee. We'll have plenty for a chapter."

MOUSY,

MOUSY

Mousy, mousy
In the housy

Are you pretty
Are you frowsy?

Will you court
And will you wed

Or will you hide
Beneath your bed?

Can you cook and
Can you sing

Can you please
A mousy king?

Father looked down from his platform. "Momma, what is *that* from?"

"From no place, dear. I'm afraid it just popped into my head. I haven't found much poetry, so I guess I just made

up my own. Oh, my. I don't mean to be frivolous, I . . ."

"Never hurt at all, a little frivolity! What good is hard, serious work without a little lightness to go with it? Recite it again."

She did.

"Well, I believe I like it. Yes. But tell me, why is it, 'Can you cook and can you *sing?*' Why not—oh—*sew?* Or *scrub?*"

"What good is hard, serious work without a little lightness?" she replied with a grin.

"Mousy, mousy, nonsense!" growled Dimblehauser. He crouched down in the dark on a shelf of the 591.5s and grumbled, and the next thing he knew Doolan had left his platform and the whole family was scurrying around below, shouting something about a university professor. Elmo had dragged a book off the bottom shelf and it lay open on the floor.

"Why, isn't this delightful," said Mother as she scanned the page beneath her. "And it *was* written by a professor." (He was a professor of physiology from Cincinnati and his first name was Gustav.)

Mother read some of the story aloud.

Oh, come now, thought Dimblehauser. This is a bit thick. Who ever heard of a professor writing such drivel about mice! I'm quite sure a professor has better things to do with his time.

"What a little hoarder that wife was," Father said.

"Some wives are like that," replied Mother, knowing exactly how that little mouse felt as she collected pencils and all the professor's belongings from the top of his desk and hid them away in her own desk-drawer home.

Father only smiled as he thought how the poor mouse-husband must have felt watching his busy wife.

The professor wrote:

[She] is in possession of all, immediately bringing her belongings, really his belongings and my belongings—one leap from the top [of the desk] to where I drive my distracted pen, another leap to the drawer, and thereafter subterranean grumblings and thuds and perturbations.

He cannot understand it. How could she be so material? What can she think of doing with it all? What does she dream?

I cannot understand either—his bedding, his food, my pencil, my pens, the cork of my ink bottle, the eraser with the chewable rubber at one end and the chewable tuft of brush at the other. Hour after hour diagonally across my work she goes, head held high to keep what she carries above her flying feet. In human distances it must be twenty miles. Certainly more than the tiny burnings of that tiny body drive that machine.

"Fancy a university professor writing so—so personally about us," Mother said.

Fancy is very likely what it is, thought Dimblehauser. Mouse fancy! He stepped right out onto Father's platform and looked over the side, bold as brass. *No one* could believe that people would write such stories about mice. No one. His beady eyes flashed and his antennae trembled with indignation.

"This will be a fine thing to include in our book," Father said. "It shows that . . ."

Book! Mouse book! Oh, fap! Dimblehauser couldn't stand the idea another minute. Even the sight of those twitching mouse whiskers and those floppy mouse tails was more than he could bear. He turned around, nearly fell over Father's box of cards, and climbed angrily up the back of the bookstack.

The Doolans had turned the pages and were just admiring a picture of a jerboa made of clay, who came from Egypt, was four thousand years old, and belonged to the Metropolitan Museum of Art in New York City. Suddenly there was a terrible crash above them. "Look out!" Father shouted, but no one had time to duck: cards rained down on them like snow and the box caught Elmo sharply on the temple. The platform hung drunkenly by one rope. They thought they heard a small gruff laugh. Elmo saw a shadow slip away. "Get him!" Elmo and Father tore off after the fleeing form, with Mother and Midge close behind them.

"Head him off, head him off," yelled Father. "You go that way, Elmo." Dimblehauser dodged, but always, wherever he turned, there was a Doolan. He dashed between rows of shelves, tore up one side of Miss Gurney's desk, and ended in a partly open drawer.

He crept over the back of the drawer and down into the one below and lay very still under a bundle of book cards. Elmo dove into the open drawer right after Father. They would have found Dimblehauser at once if Elmo hadn't slipped. Crash, down he went on something as slick as glass. He picked it up to keep the others from falling. He stared at it, carried it to the front of the drawer, and held it up to the moonlight.

Down in the drawer below, Father was just about to look under the stack of book cards when he heard Elmo shout. He ran up to see what was the matter.

"Look what I found! Wow! Now I know what that machine is. You'll *never* guess, Father. Look at this!"

It was dark and shiny and no bigger than a postage stamp. It was a newspaper, small enough for a mouse. Father held it up to the moonlight. It weighed less than an ounce, it was easy to handle, it was delightful. It was a copy of the *Times-Herald*. "Why in the world would people make a newspaper this size?" Father said. "Surely it can't be meant for a mouse!"

The Doolans crowded round and read it all. When they were quite finished Elmo took it up to the top of the machine and slipped it under the glass. Then he jumped down onto Miss Gurney's letters and flipped the switch. "Look in the cave," Elmo said.

They looked. They gasped. Father was astounded, for there on the floor of the cave was the same newspaper, with print big enough for people to read.

"Why, it's magic," said Mother. "Why, the writing on that little thing is no bigger than my own."

Father stared at Mother. Then he climbed up beside Elmo. He took his gold toothpick out of his pocket, and on a corner of the microfilm which stuck out under the glass, he wrote a few words in his fine Spencerian script. Then he pushed the film farther under the glass. Below, on the floor of the cave, appeared Father's words, large enough for people to read: *A mouse is a mouse is a mouse.*

Everyone was silent for a long, long moment. In each Doolan head the same idea was stirring. They looked at one another with round, shining eyes. Each thought the idea over, considered it.

It was little Midge who blurted it out. "Father! If people can read mouse writing, then people can read your book."

"Why, it's something to think about," Father said. "People could, all right, but—"

"They could, Father. It's microfilm. I saw the box in the drawer. You could copy it on blank microfilm."

"But would people—"

"Of course they'd want it!" Mother said. "My good-ness, my dear, they would be thrilled. They would have the only book of its kind in the world. A book about mice by a mouse. And hand written!"

No one wondered until later where they were to find blank microfilm. No one wondered until later what had become of Dimblehauser. No one knew how dreadfully jealous he was, scrunched down under the cards muttering to himself, "Book for *people?* A book about mice—for *people? Oh—the audacity!*"

A COCKROACH

HAS NO

CHILDHOOD

AT ALL

Dimblehauser's rooms were dark and fusty. He crept through the door into the kitchen and through to the bedroom and got into his rumpled bed. He hunched down under the covers, stuffed his antennae under the pillow, and gave himself up to hateful black thoughts.

Finally he sat up, threw his pillow to the floor, and stared into the darkness. "If those silly fools can *play* at writing a book, then I can write a real book! An important book, about cockroaches!" He picked up his pillow and fluffed it.

"Yes! That's what I'll do. For I am a true artist! Just you wait, you stupid mice, and see what old Dimblehauser can do! While you muddle around with your stupid cards, I'll show you!" He put his head on his pillow and went right off to sleep in his dark little hole in the wall.

When Dimblehauser woke in the morning he got some discarded, dirty paper out of the wastebasket, and found a stub of a pencil which was very dull.

He scrunched down in his chair and tried to think what to write, but his mind seemed utterly blank. He squirmed and wriggled and got chocolate on his feelers from the dirty papers. He began to feel sticky and irritable.

Finally, in terrible desperation, he remembered something he had heard someone say: "Write about what you know."

So he wrote about the way a cockroach can hear with his tail, and how he has two sets of jaws, both with teeth

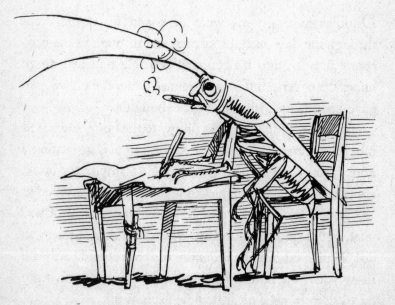

and one with a little brush which he uses for cleaning his antennae. He wrote about how, inside him, he has a built-in clock for telling the time of day and, perhaps even more remarkable, a third set of teeth in his stomach.

He wrote about how it feels to hatch from the egg and find oneself tightly packed among one's brothers and sisters in the egg case. And how, when the case bursts open, the newborn cockroaches are cast out into the world and expected to go about making their own living at once. Never a cradle or a lullaby or a bottle of warm milk has a young cockroach. Why, a cockroach, thought Dimblehauser sadly, really has no childhood at all.

But when he had finished with everything he could think of about the life of a cockroach, there wasn't any more. There is no adventure to it, thought Dimblehauser.

He tried to invent daring feats and ingenious plots, but for some reason they just went flat. He tried a travel story, but he couldn't seem to imagine the way it would be, he couldn't get any color into it. He had no facts with which to begin, nothing to build on.

Finally he gave up, ate some stale biscuit, and got wearily into bed. Why was it that mice had such wonderful adventures, and cockroaches had none at all? How was it those dreadful Doolans were enjoying themselves, while he was so miserable?

Perhaps there was something in those books upstairs. Perhaps he could find cockroach adventures there. He climbed out of bed, grabbed up some paper, and crept up-stairs to the catalogue.

He found the COB–COZ drawer, glanced around fur-tively, then flipped the cards forward one by one until he got to *Cockroach—Extermination*. That was the one and only subject heading. There was no other.

The cards described the books in some detail. These were not joyful cockroach adventures, these were books of murder.

Dimblehauser could have gone on to other subject head-ings. He could have dashed to the *Reader's Guide* and hunted out the magazines which might have given him an entirely different and interesting view. But he knew none of these things. Dimblehauser was defeated; all hope was gone. He had used up his own small store of knowledge and there was no more to be had. The whole world was against him.

THIEF!

Dimblehauser woke the next morning feeling dreadful. He moped around in the dark of his hole until lunch time. After lunch he felt so tired, so exhausted, that all he could do was to lie down and take a long nap. After dinner he felt much the same way.

But some small spark of hope fluttered feebly within Dimblehauser. Perhaps I have missed something about how to find what I want in those books! The Doolans know the secret! The Doolans know what to do!

He put on his old woolen scarf, climbed the stairs, crossed the Reading Room, and slunk into the shadows of the 591.96s to watch. What a fuss those Doolans were making! All four of them were there. They were shouting and simply carrying on. Dimblehauser began to get angry all over again. Why, what they were shouting was incredible! Dimblehauser couldn't believe his ears. Quickly he climbed the stack and peered down upon the Doolans.

"Flying mice! Flying mice!" they were shouting.

"Flying mice! Flying mice! Mice can fly!"

"Not just squirrels. *Mice too.*"

"They are mice! *Idiurus* are mice!"

"If Mr. Durrell says mice, then mice they are!" Father said.

"I had no idea," exclaimed Mother, reading the description, "that it would be so—so—so truly flying. Oh, my."

"And the picture!" cried Midge. "Oh, look at them." She leaped into the air, waving her arms, and Father grabbed Mother and danced a jig with her.

Dimblehauser glared down at the scene. He too could read Gerald Durrell's words, see the picture. But it isn't true, he said to himself. *No mouse can fly!*

From the top of the stack Dimblehauser read how Mr. Durrell had searched the jungles of Africa for the rare flying mice. (Fake, thought Dimblehauser. Fake and nonsense.) Then he read how the author had found them in their home in a gigantic hollow tree. (Fap! Mice don't live in trees.) With smoke from a dampened fire, Mr. Durrell had driven them out. Mr. Durrell recalled the scene thus:

The flight of the flying mice I shall remember until my dying day. The great tree was encircled by shifting columns of grey smoke that turned to the most ethereal blue where the great bars of sunlight stabbed through it. Into this the *Idiurus* launched themselves.

They left the trunk of the tree without any apparent effort; one minute they were clinging spread-eagled to the bark, the next they were in the air. Their tiny legs were stretched out, and the membranes along their sides were taut. They swooped and drifted through the tumbling clouds of smoke with all the assurance and skill of hawking swallows, twisting and banking with incredible skill and little or no movement of the body. This was pure gliding, and what they achieved with it was astonishing.

Elmo held out his arms and looked at them, then stuck forth his foot and imagined great membranes of skin between arm and leg, making wings. Mouse wings. It was a delightful idea. And it was true. Somewhere in Africa right now, some boy-mouse was soaring from a treetop out into the wild, free sky.

I saw one leave the trunk of the tree at a height of about thirty feet [continued Mr. Durrell]. It glided across the dell in a straight, steady swoop and landed on a tree about a hundred and fifty feet away, losing little, if any, height in the process. . . . Their ability in the air amazed me, for there was no breeze in the forest to set up the air currents I should have thought essential for such intricate manoeuvring.

"Think of it," Mother said. "Gliding among the giant

trees, free and agile as birds!" It was a thrilling find, per-haps the most thrilling of all.

But Dimblehauser said to himself, They are crazy. Why, those Doolans would believe anything. No mouse can fly! No mouse at all can do that! He was so mad he nearly fell off the bookstack. They know I am here, and they are putting me on! They are pretending it's true. He almost jumped down into the midst of the Doolans to call them on their despicable game.

But he had a better idea.

Late, late that night, after the Doolans had had their mid-night supper, packed up the basket and cards, and gone downstairs to snuggle in their beds, Dimblehauser crept out of his dark crack and sneaked through the shadows of the workroom and went in the Doolans' front door.

He had a time finding his way. He stumbled over the sofa and by mistake got into the kitchen. Here he had a little snack, for Mother had left a cake on the table. Out again, and down the hall. He opened the first door he came to, quietly, very quietly, and he closed it again right away—it was somebody's bedroom. I wonder, he thought, if they keep it in there? The next room held Midge's bed, but the third door showed him, in the pale light, Father's desk, scattered with papers.

He searched the room from top to bottom. No box was there. Well then, he thought to himself, it must be in Doolan's bedroom.

Thief!

Quietly he went, and quietly he opened the door. No one stirred. Father snored a little in the big double bed. In the drawer of the night table, Dimblehauser found the box of note cards. Carefully he removed it and crept out again, shutting the door behind him.

THERE
STOOD
DOOLAN

Dimblehauser took the box down to his dark little hole. He set it on the table next to the bread and stared at it. Then he took out a handful of cards. Very slowly and deliberately, he tore the cards in half.

He grinned fiendishly and ripped them again.

He tore them all. Then he threw them in a heap on the floor and tossed the box on top of them. He smiled with satisfaction and took himself off to bed.

But once he was nicely tucked under the covers, he wasn't able to sleep. He turned and tossed, and the shadows around him took on a fearful aspect. When he did fall asleep, exhausted, he had terrible dreams.

He woke tangled in his covers and cowering with fear. It seemed to him that ghostly shapes stood about in the darkness. He pulled the covers up around him and trembled. "Speak up," he cried into the dark night. "What do you want? Devils or mice, what do you want of me? I have done nothing wrong."

From the depths of the night he heard, or thought he heard, a whispered answer, "Have you not, Dimblehauser? Have you not?"

He lay there trembling with fear until the morning light began to creep in, and he could see that he was quite, quite alone in his bedroom.

He got up, wrapped shivering in his robe, and went to make himself some hot tea, looking, as he went, in all the cracks and closets for something, for someone hiding there.

But what of Father, what of the Doolans when they woke that morning and found the box gone? There were tears, and a great cloud of blackness settled over the household. Oh, they had been so close to being finished. Now it was all to be done over.

"Maybe it was a stranger passing through," Mother said weakly.

"A stranger?" said Father.

"No human could reach in here," said Midge.

"No one lives in the library but us and you-know-who," said Elmo.

Well the work had to be done again, and they started that evening—going back, retracing their steps—while Dimblehauser, unknown to them, sat in his kitchen staring at the pile of torn cards and hating to see night come.

The Doolans supped quietly before their midnight fire. Midge cried a little—she was cross and tired and discouraged. They all felt sad; it was a dreadful thing that had happened, and though by midnight they had replaced many cards, there was still a long way to go. "It's more exciting," said Elmo, "doing it for the first time." Well, it was, they all admitted it. But it was work to be done, and there was no choice but to do it.

Mother poured more cocoa and they tried hard to cheer one another. When they felt a little better they took the box and the supper basket and went down the marble stairs and into their warm house and to bed.

And Dimblehauser stayed up all night, for he was afraid to go to bed.

Father, when he woke, stood in the living room buttoning his vest and gazing out the open door at the workroom. He thought sadly of the great load of work which lay ahead, and he thought bitterly how hard it was for the children. As he watched the workroom turn lighter Father made a decision.

It was very early. He had heard Miss Gurney come in and go upstairs. He had not seen her pause, lay a book tenderly on the table, and smile with secret pleasure.

Father turned, strode into the kitchen, spoke to Mother, and went out the back door.

Mother stood in the kitchen, flour on her paws, looking worried.

Father went straight to Dimblehauser's door and knocked loudly. Dimblehauser heard the knock plain and clear. With his shattered nerves, it took him right out of his chair.

He grabbed the wastebasket and started shoving the cards into it.

Again came the insistent knock.

He pushed the wastebasket into the cupboard, grabbed up two more pieces off the floor, threw those in, and jammed his laundry down on top.

Again the knock.

His nerves were so shattered he could think of nothing to do but answer the door.

There stood Doolan.

Dimblehauser's antennae trembled. He tried to say good morning, but he only gulped.

Father stared at him. A hard, steady mouse stare.

Dimblehauser stepped back into the room. Doolan stepped in, still close to him, eyes steady.

"I—," Dimblehauser began.

"Where are the cards?"

Dimblehauser's usual aplomb was utterly destroyed. He gulped again, turned, and went into the kitchen. His antennae hung limply. He opened the cupboard, took out the wastebasket, removed his laundry, and held the basket out to Father.

Father looked in, then looked at Dimblehauser. "Do you expect me to take them like this?"

Dimblehauser stood there with his mouth open.

"Clear the table," Father said.

Dimblehauser did, piling bread and dirty dishes in the sink.

"Wipe it clean."

He did.

"Now, before the rest of the staff arrives, we will go out into the library and get a roll of tape."

They did that, and when they got back Father sat down and made himself comfortable. "Now start putting the pieces together."

And Dimblehauser did.

By evening the cards were all back together, taped and sorted.

Father arrived home tired and thoroughly content, with the box under his arm.

He was greeted in the kitchen by two hugging, laughing children. They were so thrilled to have the cards back. And something else—something they were trying to tell him. But they were all talking at once, even Mother.

Finally Mother held out some cards, and Father sat down to see what in the world was so exciting.

Mother poured him a cup of cocoa.

"Oh," said Father. "Oh, my!" The children danced around and could hardly keep still.

Well, it was Elmo who had found it. He had slipped out the front door that morning looking for Father. He thought perhaps he had gone to the table where Miss Gurney left books for him, so he had climbed up to see.

There was the book, with two markers in it.

It was brand new. Not catalogued, no card and pocket, no number on the spine. Elmo turned the pages until he got to the first marker.

This was a note about a migration of deer mice. It was

interesting, but Elmo had no cards. He leaped down and ran into the house to get some.

He took his notes quickly and briefly, then turned to the second marker.

He read with a growing smile, then gave a yell which brought Mother and Midge running.

"Why, whatever . . ." Mother was drying her paws on her apron. She peered over Elmo's shoulder. "Oh! Oh, my. Oh, this is too wonderful! Oh, won't Father be thrilled."

"What, what, what?" cried Midge, climbing up.

"Where is Father?" Elmo said suddenly.

Mother told him.

"Hooray for Father," shouted Elmo.

"Shhhh," said Mother. "It's getting late. Quick, let's copy. We will want to quote this."

Now Father grinned broadly as he read:

I once had a singing mouse that was inspired to sing by hearing radio music. The little voice would continue for some time after the electronic music stopped, a song very fluent and more bell-like than a canary's. During the last century . . . W. O. Hickey in the *American Naturalist* described a mouse which, having filled an overshoe in a closet with popcorn, would sit among his corn and 'sing his beautiful solo' for ten minutes at a time. 'His song was not a chirp but a continuous song of musical tone, a kind of *to-wit-to-wee-woo-woo-wee-woo*, quite varied in pitch.'

Oh, wasn't it a wonderful day! "I knew we would find something like this," Mother said.

"We might have known it would be a naturalist who would write it," replied Father. "I didn't dream, but yes, who more likely than Sally Carrighar."

That night, the Doolans packed up basket, cards, and platforms and went up the stairs singing such a song as Miss Carrighar and Mr. Hickey had never heard in their lives—four-part harmony rising and swelling sweeter than any birds had ever sung.

THE WHITE
DORMOUSE

Elmo headed for the catalogue with one thing in mind: Okefenokee Swamp. Father slung his platform in the 599s, and Mother took Midge by the paw and soon the two of them could be heard making up little tunes to

> Six little mice sat down to spin,
> Pussy passed by and she peeped in.

and

> Three blind mice, see how they run!

and

> Pretty John Watts,
> We are troubled with rats.

Elmo dug in the catalogue for Okefenokee and found nothing. Undaunted, he looked under *Swamp*. That was better! That led him to *Marshes* and to *Marsh Ecology*, and he went off with a fistful of cards. He heard Father's voice rise with excitement, but he didn't stop to see what the discovery was. He was too intent on marshes.

"Elmo would like this book," Mother said. "Couldn't we call him?"

"No," said Father, "let him be. These are the oldest dates we have found for the emergence of mouse on earth. Think of it, forty million years ago, at the dawn of the Oligocene period. And imagine, the bones of dormice found in rocks fifty million years old."

"It's nearly impossible for me to think about anything that old," Mother said.

"When I grow up I'm going to go to war with a general, in his tank, like those two mice did with General Rommel," Midge said. "What does it mean, their nest was in his personal possessions?"

"Likely between his socks and his toothbrush," Father said. "Or perhaps beneath his winter underwear. My dear, did you make cards for the business about black rat—you know, where Mr. Sanderson says he has more—"

"More common sense and stamina than man! Of course I did," Mother replied. "And this too," she said, fishing a card from the box. " 'Although Man is undeniably "top-mammal" . . . there is little doubt that some rat, and probably the brown rat . . . is actually the finest . . . product that Nature has managed to create on this planet to date.' "

Then they found white dormouse and that caused such a squeaking of delight by Midge that Elmo almost jumped down to see. He should have, for white dormouse was a very impressive fellow. He was called Common European Dormouse (semi-albino), but he did not seem common to the Doolans. He was white as snow, his tail a fluffy cloud plume.

"He is a fairy prince," Midge cried.

"Perhaps he is," mused Mother. "Perhaps in winter time he does not hibernate at all, but steals away in some magic enchantment instead."

"Perhaps," said Father, "all dormice do, prince and plain. Maybe what we think of as hibernation is really an enchantment."

For the white dormouse, for all dormice everywhere, Mother wrote:

> My house is small and I do sweep
> My hearth and hall and kitchen-keep.
>
> My larder shelves are filled and waiting
> For the winter's hibernating.
>
> Then a million miles away will I
> Go a-dreaming 'neath a sky
>
> Touched by wand of fairy queen
> Where mortal mouse has never been.

"Oh, look here!" cried Mother. "Listen to this. This

African jerboa has 'enormous, batlike ears that can be opened out like two huge, loudspeaker horns, or folded up and laid back alongside the shoulders when the animal is going in top gear.' "

"Wait, you've missed something," said Father. "Listen to this one. Jerboas 'have intrigued civilized man since the time of the earlier dynasties of the ancient Egyptian empire, whose royal artists sometimes included them in their murals in temples and tombs. From those depictions there once arose, by simplification of lines, a hieroglyph meaning *swiftness.*' "

Elmo leaned against his last book, sighed, and listened to his stomach rumble with hunger. Oh boy, he thought, all that and nothing. I thought it was going to be easy when I found out about Okefenokee. But I haven't found another thing about Golden Mouse.

Well, I did find beach mouse, though. I wonder if he knows that book called him a "pallid wraith of a beach mouse." Well, he shouldn't care. He's so exclusive he lives in only one place in the world, and that's an island!

And I sure did find out a lot about swamps! Elmo closed his eyes and thought about swinging from branch to branch above the dark swamp waters, looking down into the mouths of alligators and cottonmouth snakes.

Something touched his leg and he nearly jumped out of his skin.

"It's only me," Midge whispered. "What's the matter?"

"I thought you were an alligator. You shouldn't sneak up like that."

"Did you find lots about Golden Mouse?"

"No!" Elmo snapped. "*Not lots! Not anything!*"

"Well, maybe . . ."

"Maybe *what?* We're nearly through with the books. I've been into all the encyclopedias and read every word about Okefenokee! I've tramped around in the catalogue, and I've waded through muskrats and all kinds of swamp fellows. But no Golden Mouse!" He was almost shouting. Midge backed away and nearly fell off the platform. Elmo grabbed her. "I'm sorry," he grumbled.

"That's all right. Come on, Elmo. It's suppertime. We can go up to Mother's platform and you can see Schmurski."

"What's a Schmurski?"

When Elmo saw the picture and found out that Schmurski was a dormouse who slept in a soup tureen, he was convulsed with laughter.

"I don't see anything funny!" said Midge.

"A soup tureen! Who ever heard of sleeping in a soup tureen! What if someone decided to make soup—Schmurski soup!" This sent him into uncontrollable fits so that he had to hold his sides.

Mother glared at him. "I think she's beautiful, Elmo. And a soup tureen is really a very elegant place."

"I should love living in a soup tureen," Midge said. "I

think it would be lovely. But how would you get in and out with that great lid on?"

"Through the hole for the spoon, stupid!"

"Elmo!" That was Mother.

"Well, that's what it says," Elmo muttered.

"It doesn't say *stupid*," Mother replied.

"I should like to be a dormouse," Midge said, gazing at Schmurski's long, bushy tail and feeling her own bare tail rather sadly. "And live in a soup tureen just like a princess."

"A princess in a soup tureen!" This sent Elmo into another fit of laughter, and only Father could stop him with a sharp look and a threat of no supper if he didn't straighten up.

He straightened up at once.

But Elmo was quiet at supper and sat off by himself, away from the fire. We're almost finished now, he thought. And not nearly enough about Golden Mouse for a chapter. Well, there are still the magazines.

But when Mother said, "There are still the magazines, Elmo," it only made him angry.

And when Father said, "At least we know he's real!" that made him angrier still. But he held his tongue, though he went to bed all in a flap, sure beyond doubt that the magazines would be of no use whatever.

GOLDEN

MOUSE

AT LAST

Elmo felt so grouchy the next morning, he stumped up the stairs in absolute silence. Midge raced ahead, helter-skelter. "Where *are* the magazines, Father?"

Father pointed to the Periodical Room. Away she went.

When the family caught up she was standing in the center of the room looking perplexed. "There aren't any magazines here, only those big black books, and there's no catalogue, either. You said—"

Father twitched a whisker. "We're in the right place, honey. The magazines are all bound into those big black books, and Midge, there isn't any catalogue."

"But you said the *Reader's Guide* would show where to find mice in the magazines! So it must be a catalogue!"

"It works like a catalogue. Come see." Father took her paw and helped her up onto a big table which stood against a bookstack with rows of great green volumes. The spines said *Reader's Guide to Periodical Literature*. Each told the years it covered.

Soon they had three volumes down and open. Midge hung over Elmo's shoulder as he searched the headings for animal, mice, mouse, rat, and rodent. All the time he was thinking to himself, There won't be a thing. I know it.

Dimblehauser paused in a dark shadow and looked out at the Doolans. He had on his cap and his old scarf round his shoulders. Over one shoulder he carried a stick on which a bundle was tied.

He watched the Doolans at work. Through one of the tall windows he saw the moon low in the sky. He looked around at the softly lighted Periodical Room, at the great tables and chairs and rows of bound magazines. Through an arch into the Reference Room he could see the microfilm reader gleaming dully in the moonlight. Dimblehauser felt lonely and sad.

But he felt excited too. For Dimblehauser had made up his mind. He was off on his own adventure. He would travel. And maybe he would—well, perhaps, out there in the world, he could find—well, perhaps he would be less lonely.

He watched the Doolans a little longer. Then he slipped out through the Reading Room and down the stairs, through the mending and lettering rooms, and out the hole in the wall.

In the Periodical Room, the Doolans huffed and pulled and strained to get the first bound volume of magazines out and onto the platform. It was much bigger than any encyclopedia. And heavier! The platform began to bend. "Push it back," Father cried as the cardboard sagged dangerously. They pushed.

Finally they had it safely back on the shelf. They put the three platforms together, one on top of the other, one hanger over the other. That was better! They got the volume out and open, and Mother stayed to help Father turn pages. Elmo and Midge went back to the *Reader's Guide*.

"Would it say Golden Mouse?" Midge wondered as they began again to search.

"I don't know. I guess it depends."

"On what?"

"On how much—"

He was interrupted by Father's loud cry of, "Mouse skins!"

They stared across the room at him. Mother was standing on the open magazine looking shocked, but Father was elated and making notes very fast.

"What did he say?" Midge whispered.

"Mouse skins!" Elmo repeated.

"Listen!" Father shouted from across the room. "On a cuneiform text, in Sumer! A list of animal skins, and among them—" Mother was whispering something in his ear. "Oh, that's all right, Mother, my goodness, we're used to things like that by this time. But it shows—it puts us in a civilization older than ancient Egypt! It puts us in the earliest civilization on earth! Listen, among the skins listed were 'mouse, garden dormouse, brown rat, field mouse, vole, variegated mouse, rat.'"

"But skins!" Mother whispered.

"We were important to the people then," Father answered.

Midge shuddered. The children got back to work. Elmo turned the pages from *Animal* through to the *M*'s. Then he clutched Midge's paw. Both stared at the page. Neither could say a word. They could not shout, they could only gaze at the entry.

Mice, "Search for the Golden Mouse."

"*Aud—Aud—Audubon Magazine*," Elmo whispered finally. He scribbled the date of the magazine, leaped off the platform, and raced round the stacks to the *A*'s. Midge was right on his heels.

Then they raced back to Father. "The platform, the platform!" they screamed.

Father looked down at them, saw their expressions, and shouted, "Golden Mouse! Is it? Is it?"

"Yes! Hurry!"

They struggled with the ropes and tangled them in their frantic hurry, then half dragged, half carried the platforms along to the *A*'s. They hung the hangers over the top and it all seemed to take forever.

Finally they had the volume out. They turned and turned the pages, issue after issue all bound together. Pages of advertising, pages and pages, but at last they got to the March-April edition. "What page?" Father said.

Elmo looked at his note. He had forgotten to write down the page number. "Oh, drat!"

"Well, the table of contents then."

"Yes."

They all peered at it. There it was, *Search for the Golden Mouse*, page 96. They turned to it.

"There!"

SEARCH FOR THE GOLDEN MOUSE, by John K. Terres.

"There are photographs!"

"But not in color!"

"*Turn the page!*"

Then, "Oooooohhhhh," they all cried. There he was. *In color.* And what color! He was shimmering gold. His rich color glinted with hints of silver and copper mixed into the shining golden fur. He shone "bright as the sun," Midge whispered. His ears, caught in the light, were nearly transparent. He was a rare and beautiful creature.

The article began just exactly as one would want it to. "You see, you see!" Elmo shouted as they read. "It says, *fabled . . . mythical.*"

I first heard of the Golden Mouse in 1927. It seemed a fabled animal—more mythical than real. A tiny creature of shimmering golden fur, it was said to have pink, handlike feet that gripped the vines and lianas of the moonlit Southern woodlands where it scampered about in the night, like a miniature squirrel, seldom descending to earth.

They read eagerly. Elmo was holding his breath. When they got to the bottom of page 99 they knew that there was not one, but four species of Golden Mouse, and the first had been "discovered in Dismal Swamp."

"Dismal Swamp!" Elmo said.

"And the next one was discovered by Audubon," said Father.

"And it says Theodore Roosevelt admired them," Mother said.

"Who was he?" That was Midge.

"My goodness, child. He was President of the United States. Haven't I taught you a thing?"

The third species of Golden Mouse was not known about by a single human until nearly a hundred years later, and the fourth one was discovered just after him "in Delight, Arkansas," Mother said. "Wouldn't you know he would live in a place called Delight! Why he builds two houses. Two different kinds. And he lives in them both!" Mother thought this was a wonderful luxury.

"But two houses to clean," Midge said.

"Still, think how lovely," Mother replied. She read it all again; how one domed nest was built snug and waterproof, as home and nursery. It might be fifteen feet above the ground, hidden and protected, perhaps in a thorny green-brier bush. Its round roof was tightly thatched with leaves and grass. The warm interior was softly lined with the down from milkweed pods, with rabbit fur, and with the feathers of wild birds.

The second nest rose high and airy, some fifty feet from the ground. It was "a retreat and a dining room," a high platform where Golden Mouse stored the food he gathered during the night. Here he could dine in the daytime in safety and privacy.

"What a view he must have," Mother said. "Oh, to dine with a view!"

Elmo was reading on. "Yes! Here. It says Golden Mouse builds his domed house on top of an old bird's nest. That was in my other notes. Listen: 'They roof the nests of the cardinal and the yellow-breasted chat.'"

"They use their tails in climbing," Midge said. "I can't do that."

Nor could any of the Doolans.

"And the Golden Mouse in the picture lived with the author," Mother exclaimed.

The article ended with the author taking that Golden Mouse back to the forest and watching him "disappear in a flash of gold under the leaves of the forest floor."

"So he lives in the forest, too. Not only swamp," Father mused.

"Forests and honeysuckle patches and greenbrier thickets," Mother said.

As the moonlight shone in on them, and on the Golden Mouse, the Doolans wrote two more verses to the "Song of the Golden Mouse." They wrote them, and they sang them in the moonlight, and the song was sweet, so sweet.

In a thatched and woven nest
    Feathery, furry,
Tiny golden babies rest
    Safely and warmly.
See them shine like specks of sunlight—
      Who can they be?
    Sing of the Golden Mouse, O,
    Moonlight caught upon his coat
    Sing of the Golden Mouse, O,
    Moonlight on his coat.

Through Dismal Swamp in thicket dense
    Thorny and darkling,
Through Delight like sun a-racing
    Golden and sparkling,
Leaps a shining, fabled mouse-myth—
      Who can he be?
    Follow the Golden Mouse, O,
    Moonlight caught upon his coat
    Follow the Golden Mouse, O,
    Moonlight on his coat.

ELMO'S

MICROFILM

So at last the research was finished. The magazines had given the Doolans not only the Golden Mouse article and the record of mouse skins from Sumer, but also "Dipo." That was from the name of the article, "Meet Dipo." He was the bannertail kangaroo rat of the genus *Dipodomys*.

He could leap ten feet at a jump, his tail twirling madly as he sailed. " 'Like a toy rocket hurtling through space with a propeller in the rear,' " Elmo read.

" 'He reminds one of a child on a Pogo stick,' " Midge quoted.

His feet are built like snowshoes to carry him over the sand. He is a remarkable fellow.

With Dipo they were finished. All the notes had been taken, the research completed. Golden Mouse would have his own chapter. The Doolans gazed at one another with contentment and joy, and with drooping eyelids. Midge yawned.

The Doolans slept the clock around.

Father rose fresh, excited, eager to begin the writing. "We must see that he has quiet and solitude so he can do his very best work," Mother said to Elmo and Midge. The children nodded solemnly.

Father shut himself in his study, cleared his desk, put down a fresh blotter, and sharpened all his pencils. He stood them in a little brown jar. He adjusted his chair, got a new candle, and laid out a great stack of fresh paper.

He reviewed the cards; he thought about them. He tried different chapter outlines and rearranged the cards several times to follow the outlines. He considered, he cogitated, and sometimes Father just let his mind wander where it would.

When he was entirely satisfied with the arrangement of the subjects, he began to write the book.

"Microfilm," Elmo muttered. "Microfilm. Where am I going to find blank microfilm? Does it come to the library blank, or already written on?" This had not occurred to him before. "The trouble is, I don't know—well, I don't know very much at all about microfilm." Then he jumped up. "Of course! Why didn't I think of that!"

He was halfway up the stairs, dragging a platform, when Midge skittered up behind him. "Where are you going? What are you going to do?"

They climbed to the encyclopedias, slung the platform,

and wrestled out the METAL *to* MUSICAL volume of *Collier's.*
"It's nice to be back upstairs," Midge said.

"Micro—micro—" Elmo muttered, turning the pages.
"Here! *Microphotography!* Photography uses film!"

They got out the NUMBER *to* PHRYGIA volume and
looked up *Photography.* "Yes, I think a photographic negative would do," Elmo said. "Here, '. . . light that has
passed through the negative . . .' "

"Elmo?"

"Hmmm?" He was still reading.

"Where would we get a photographic negative?"

It was true. Negatives would be every bit as hard to find
as microfilm. Elmo thought for a while. They took the
platform down. Midge said, "I'm hungry."

"I'm hungry, too, but—*the alley!*"

"What?"

"Trash! Spoiled negatives."

They pelted down the stairs, dropped the platform, and
barreled out the hole to the alley.

It seemed like hours later that they trudged back upstairs, tired and discouraged.

They climbed down into the wastebaskets and rum-
maged around. Elmo found a piece of cellophane. He tried
writing on it, and he tried covering it with black ink from
a felt marker, then scratching words onto it with a pin.
That worked pretty well. Then he tried the same thing on
transparent tape. That was better. The sticky surface held

the ink. But it was not good enough; he could not get it covered properly. The light came through in streaks.

Then they went rummaging in desk drawers. Together they pried them open and tracked around over paper and envelopes and stamps.

And over a stack of carbon paper.

Elmo examined a sheet. The edge of the paper, where there was no carbon, was rather transparent. He scratched on the carbon. He wrote ELMO DOOLAN on it with a pin. He tore off the part he had written on and held it up to the light.

He ran up the machine and pushed the paper under the glass.

The writing showed plainly on the lighted floor: ELMO DOOLAN.

He pulled it out and looked at it. His paws were smeared with carbon. But it worked! It worked beautifully! It was almost as good as real microfilm.

"But how can we keep it from smearing?" Midge smudged the last letter with her paw.

"We've got to cover it with something." He looked at the transparent tape. "I don't think this will stick to carbon." He pulled off a piece. "Hey, it does! It sticks!" He rubbed it down good and tight. It sure did stick. Now the carbon looked almost like real microfilm. Elmo put it back in the reader. It still said, quite plainly, ELMO DOOLAN.

Midge sat looking at him with wonderful admiration.

Together they raced downstairs and flung right into Father's study and interrupted him in the middle of a sentence. They screamed the news to him, and Midge waved the carbon paper in his face.

"Hooray!" Father cried, hugging Elmo and Midge so hard they couldn't breathe. "Hooray! Mother, come see what Elmo has done!"

INKY

FOOTPRINTS

When the first draft of Father's book was finished, he corrected it, rewrote parts of it, polished every paragraph until it was the finest work he could do. Then he made a final clean copy. He copied that, in his fine Spencerian script, onto Elmo's "microfilm." It looked beautiful.

"Let's just take it upstairs and see how it looks in the reader," Mother said.

"But do you think—"

"My dear, you made this copy to go in the reader so that people *might* read it. Do let's see how it looks!" Mother hustled him toward the stairs.

Father and Mother and Midge stood at the edge of the cave while Elmo pushed the switch. The light shone on faces full of delight as they gazed with wonder at the first page of Father's book, made large enough for people to read.

"Harrrumph," came a voice from the dark Reading Room.

"That's Dimblehauser," whispered Mother. "He's come back."

"Fap! Never saw mice disappear so completely. Got to be up here somewhere."

"Why is he looking for us?" Elmo whispered. But Father was laughing.

"Terrible wet weather. And it's cold as sin in this library."

Father doubled up with laughter, and so did Elmo. "Same old Dimblehauser," said Father softly.

"Mud in the alley, mud in the fields, and where there isn't mud, there's concrete."

"Honey, did you wipe your feet?"

Honey? Dimblehauser? And such a soft, feminine voice. The Doolans peered down, and there, standing in the moonlit Reading Room, was the old cockroach, and beside him a cockroach lady who smiled at him with tenderness.

"He's gotten himself a wife," Father whispered. And that was exactly what he had done. The new Mrs. Dimblehauser was young and charming, and if the Doolans wondered privately how old Dimblehauser had managed that, they didn't say a word.

When Dimblehauser spied the Doolans, he and his bride climbed right up and seated themselves on Miss Gurney's eraser. "We met in a flooded hubcap," said Mrs. Dimblehauser. "I had fallen in while doing my laundry, and Dimblehauser jumped in and rescued me. It was so romantic."

Dimblehauser smiled foolishly. I wonder, Elmo thought, if newlyweds are always so silly.

"And how do you like your new home?" Mother was saying.

"Well, I have to admit, it *is* dark," said Mrs. Dimblehauser. "But I think with a good scrubbing, and some nice new dimity curtains and perhaps a little paint, I can—"

A huge shadow fell across the desk. The Dimblehausers leaped for the floor, Father pushed Mother into a bookshelf and turned to grab Midge, but she was not there. Father dashed around a pile of papers one way, Elmo ran around the other, they nearly collided, but no Midge.

"On top," Elmo panted, and there she was, her tail hanging over the stack of papers, staring at the shadow as if she did not know which way to run.

"Jump!" Elmo hissed as loudly as he dared. "Hurry!"

She did. She landed with a crash on the edge of the ink pad. It flew into the air and smeared her feet with ink. Father grabbed her paw and they ran for the shelves. As they raced away, Midge's little mouse feet printed themselves out behind her across Miss Gurney's green blotter.

Miss Gurney, having left her work neatly stacked on her desk, had gone home to dinner, observing that the sky looked like snow. She had a hot shower, put on some woolen slacks and a sweater, filled a thermos with coffee, then walked back to the library to finish her work.

It was late, the streets were empty and the moon just nicely up when she unlocked the workroom door, locked it behind her, and walked up the marble stairs making no noise at all in her soft shoes.

When she came through the arch to the Reference Room, her shadow, long in the moonlight, fell upon the Doolans.

She did not see them, but she heard them, and she paused. She looked all around, but as nothing more stirred, she went to the desk and sat down. There, very plain upon the blotter, were Midge's inky footprints.

Miss Gurney sat very still. She traced the little footprints with her finger, and it seemed to Elmo that she made a mighty effort not to look up into the bookstacks where the Doolans might be hiding. Then she saw the little box that contained Father's manuscript.

Her expression changed to puzzlement. She's wondering where that came from, Elmo thought. She doesn't recognize the box. She's turning on the machine!

"She's turning on the machine!" Mother whispered. Elmo grinned and nodded. Father turned pale.

Miss Gurney was about to put a page of the strange-looking microfilm into the machine when she saw there already was one.

"She's reading it! She's reading Father's book," Elmo whispered.

"Shhh," said Mother. She put her paw on Father's arm. "Here, dear, you'd better sit down."

Miss Gurney's eyes grew very wide. She read that page, then put in the next. "By E.P.W. Doolan, *Mus.*," she whispered. She looked again at the little inky footprints and this time she did glance up into the bookstacks as if she couldn't help herself. But she didn't see the Doolans. Her eyes were soft and bright with wonder. She put in the next page, and the next, and she read with growing excitement.

And this is what she read—this was the first chapter of the book about mice by a mouse, the first of its kind in the world:

Four thousand years ago in Sumer a scholar sat before his clay tablet and carved small figures into it. Long after the sun had sunk into the desert lands, he carved the cuneiform figures of his language.

What he carved was a record, and among the figures he set down was a list of animal skins which had been cured and stored by his people. Among those skins, the smallest ones draw our attention, for they are the skins of mouse and his cousins.

From the door a live mouse looked in at the scholar and watched him carving there; he did not know what it was the figures meant and finally went away to his own business. But the record was made, and unknown to the scholar or to the mouse, it would find its way down through time—down the thousands of years yet to come—making, with countless other records of the history of man and his activities, another record, intertwined with man's own. So the Sumerian unknowingly added his symbols to the historical record of mouse.

And in Egypt, an artist painted upon the wall of a tomb, his light a burning oil pot set near him. In the hunting scene he created, wild ducks rose from a papyrus thicket, and amidst the stems was a large and handsome mouse. Did he hunt as the cat climbing above him did, or was he merely a spectator? Whichever the case, he was an honored animal to be so included in this important painting for an Egyptian tomb.

Elsewhere in Egypt, another artist sketched a humorous scene on a small piece of clay. He smiled as he drew an elaborately dressed mouse who stood observing the chastisement of a human child by a cat.

So these artists add their records to the history of mouse as it spins itself down through the ages. Even in Egypt's written language mouse has been influential, for at one time a hieroglyph meaning "swiftness" was designed from the shape of a mouse.

As we speak of mouse here, the reader must know that rats and other cousins have been included. The researcher finds it particularly interesting that some families are even now in the process of change, while others have been only recently discovered and classifications created for them. The reader will find that when a family change has occurred it has very likely been the direct result of travel and migration. Mice who have discovered and settled new parts of the world have often formed new and distinctive species, and man, coming upon them later, can only guess how they traveled so far, and by what route.

The travels of mice, their migrations over the great continents, the records of how they have lived, the discovery of new species and new information about them—these things have occupied man in a modest way as he has gone about the making of his own history. And often man has taken the paw of mouse and stepped into the realm of imagination with him, creating mouse heroes in his stories and setting mouse and his cousins on canvas or paper or stone, so as to immortalize him.

So the record of mousedom spins itself into the fabric of the history of man, and we will follow it down through the years, beginning fifty million years ago, when dormouse first walked this earth.

When Miss Gurney got to the chapter about Golden Mouse, Elmo could tell she was charmed. She recited the words of the song softly, then she copied Father's footnote and went into the Periodical Room. "She's finding his picture," Mother whispered.

"She likes it, Father," Elmo said. "She likes your book." There was surely no doubt about that.

Father, before overcome with shyness, was beginning to look excited and pleased. "I believe—why, I believe she does like it," he said hesitantly.

"She likes it, all right," said Mother. But not one of the Doolans knew just how impressed Miss Gurney was. They did not know until much, much later. And not one of the Doolans knew how Miss Gurney spent the following days. Not one, except Elmo. When he found out, he had a terrible time keeping the secret.

A SECRET

OR A LIE?

Elmo slipped out the front door after dinner. He climbed the marble stairs and went along behind the bookstacks in a roundabout way until he got to a hiding place where he could see Miss Gurney at work.

The microfilm reader was on. Miss Gurney was typing rapidly, setting Father's words down clear and black on the fresh white paper.

Elmo had been watching Miss Gurney all week; now she was nearly finished. He had told no one. Something inside him said, Wait, don't tell. So he waited.

And during those cozy hours as he watched and listened to the friendly rhythm of the typewriter, something was happening to Elmo. In his mind, stories were beginning to take shape out of the color and richness of the research; stories which demanded his attention. As they grew in clarity, and in depth, Elmo felt a rising need to put them down on paper.

He was contemplating this when Miss Gurney finished the last page. She laid the manuscript, clean and beautiful, in a brown box exactly the right size. She typed a short letter, laid it on top, put on the lid, and then wrapped the box in brown paper.

Then she got a book from the shelf, looked up something, and wrote an address on the package.

Elmo sat on the bookshelf long after Miss Gurney had taken the package and gone home. He was a-tingle with excitement.

It was the address of a book publisher.

"What *is* the matter with Elmo?" Mother said. "He's driving me quite mad. I've never seen him so squirmy."

"Growing pains," Father said absently. He was toying with the idea of a primer for young mice, and really not paying attention to what Mother said.

But Midge was paying attention. "What *is* the matter, Elmo?" she demanded later. "You're all—fizzy!"

"I'm what?"

"You're *fizzy!* You act as if—as if you're keeping a secret! Tell me! Tell *me* what it is!"

"Nonsense. I'm—I— Oh, go away!" He shut himself in his room. He would love to have told Midge, told everybody. But he could not. Sending a book to a publisher doesn't necessarily mean it will be published. Elmo had found that out at once, through a little quick research. I can't tell and get Father all excited, then have him disappointed if they don't want to publish it. So he stayed in his room. He sat at his desk, and perhaps to escape his own jitters, or perhaps because it was the time for him to do it, Elmo began to write down the stories that were teeming and pushing to get out.

Then one morning as the workroom was slowly growing light, the shapes of desks and books still indistinct, Elmo opened the front door. He yawned, then stepped back just as the workroom door opened.

Miss Gurney stopped by Father's special table. She was wearing a new dress, pink as peppermint. Fresh. Her cheeks were flushed pink too. Her eyes sparkled.

Elmo stared at her. Miss Gurney was taking something out of her purse. A white envelope. She laid it on the table.

Then she went upstairs.

Elmo didn't hesitate. He dashed out, scrambled up the table, and read the address.

It was for E.P.W. Doolan, *Mus*. And it was from the publisher. Oh, boy, Elmo thought. Then—What if it's to say they're sending it back? But Miss Gurney wouldn't leave that kind of letter. Maybe it's only to say they received it. But it sure is a fat envelope. The flap's open, maybe if I . . . He lifted the flap and peered inside. There was a letter on top, then pages and pages of—something.

He crawled inside and read the first few words of the letter.

That was all he needed. His heart was pounding like a sledge hammer. He rolled up the envelope as best he could and headed for home with it.

By the time he had pushed the envelope into the living room he had knocked over two chairs and a table and had to climb under it to get to the hall. Then he set up such a ruckus that everyone came rushing out pale with alarm.

"Father, a letter!"

"A what?"

"A letter for you!"

Father stared at it in complete puzzlement. He looked at Elmo as if Elmo had gone quite mad, then he climbed on top of the letter and read the address. "Well, it's addressed to me," Father said. "But it—it's from—"

"Open it!" Elmo cried.

He did.

There was a letter and a contract. The contract covered the entire living room floor and half the wall. There was a place at the bottom for Father to sign.

Father was utterly and entirely overwhelmed. There is no word to accurately describe how Father felt when he realized the truth of the matter. "Our book is to be *published*? Published for people to read? Why, it will stand on the shelves of the library!"

"Of every library in the land," Mother said. "Oh, my

dear!" She threw her arms around him and kissed him on his whiskers.

Miss Gurney found the contract exactly where she had left it. Only now it was signed. And just below the signature, a few words had been written. Miss Gurney read those words, pondered upon them, mailed the contract back to the publisher, and continued to ponder.

On a moonlit night the children stood together at the front door peering through a crack into the workroom. "What's Miss Gurney doing in the workroom so late?" Midge whispered.

"She's been pacing the floor and talking to herself," Elmo replied. "I can't make it out, but she has a package, and I think— She keeps saying, 'Is it a secret, or is it a lie?' "

"What did she say?" asked Father, coming up behind them.

"I can't make out what it's all about," Elmo said. "But that package looks as if—well, I can almost see the address, if she would just put it down for a minute."

They all watched Miss Gurney with interest. Not one of the Doolans had ever seen her so unsettled. Finally she sighed, said, "Oh, dear," took a book out of the package, and laid it on the table. Then she put on her coat, went out, and locked the door.

Father was grinning. "I think I know what that was all about," he said. "She'll make the right decision. That's why I wrote the dedication as I did."

The children were utterly puzzled.

"Come on," Father said. "Get your mother, Midge."

The Doolans walked through a little path of moonlight and climbed up to the table. There it lay, bright in the shine of the moon. The first copy off the press. The most beautiful book in the world.

MOUSE
THROUGH THE AGES

BY

E. P. W. DOOLAN, *Mus.*

The jacket was bright red with the picture of Golden Mouse printed in shining gold. The title page was beautiful, every page was handsome, and there were pictures of white dormouse, of the ivory carvings, of Schmurski, pictures and more pictures, and on the end papers, printed very small, was a line of little mouse footprints.

There was a table of contents and an index and a bibliography all beautifully set in type, and the dedication read:

A well kept secret is an act of friendship.

THIS BOOK IS DEDICATED TO
A SECRET FRIEND,
WHO SURELY DOES UNDERSTAND MICE.

As Miss Gurney walked home under the stars she was thinking, A secret or a lie? Which will it be if I let people believe, as they insist on doing, that I am the real author? For that was what they did believe. She had tried to tell all the librarians, and the publishers, that she felt sure E. P. W.

Doolan was in truth a mouse. But there are some things in this world that people simply refuse to believe.

Then those words for the dedication had appeared on the contract.

Now Miss Gurney said again, "A secret or a lie? Why shouldn't E. P. W. Doolan, *Mus.*, get the credit for his book? Why should I have it?"

But what would happen if she could make people believe her? Miss Gurney shuddered to think. There would be reporters, photographers from newspapers and television, magazine people, sensation seekers. Crowds. Mice were shy, retiring folk. They wouldn't like it at all.

Such a hubbub might drive them away altogether.

At last she decided. Secret or lie, I'm not going to tell. That's the way the author wants it.

And that was the way it was. Elmo and Midge sat quietly together on a dark bookshelf and watched Miss Gurney write it all out, how she thought the research might have been done, about the microfilm (which she thought might have been made from carbon paper and tape), about the little footprints on her blotter, and about how the contract was signed and the dedication written very small at the bottom. They watched her put it in an envelope and seal it, and they watched her hide it away in a safe and secret place.

So perhaps some day people would know that *Mouse Through the Ages* was in truth a book about mice by a mouse, the first of its kind in the world. But before that time, mouse literature, like mouse music, so rare and precious a thing, would grow secretly as Father's books were published. And perhaps Elmo's stories would become part of that secret.

And never, in their long mouse lives, would the Doolans, any one of them, lose that feeling of magic as they crept up the marble stairs of the library, and the shadows moved around them and the wonders of heaven and earth beckoned to them and the moonlight shone down upon them in the silent and waiting rooms.

BOOKS

THE DOOLAN

FAMILY USED

pp. 18–22   Bertin, Leon. "Rodents (Order Rodentia)." *The Larousse Encyclopedia of Animal Life.* New York: McGraw-Hill Book Co., 1967.

pp. 25 & 28   *Encyclopedia Britannica*, 15th edition, 1968.

p. 28   *The World Book Encyclopedia*, 13th edition, 1969.

p. 29   *Collier's Encyclopedia*, 16th edition, 1969.

p. 41   Carter, T. D. et al. *Mammals of the Pacific World.* New York: The Macmillan Co., 1946.

pp. 45–47   Leach, Maria, ed. *Standard Dictionary of Folklore, Mythology, and Legend.* 2 vols. New York: Funk and Wagnalls, 1950.

p. 49   *The people of Kamchatka. . . .* Frazer, Sir James George. *The Golden Bough: A Study in Magic and Religion. Part II, Taboo and the Perils of the Soul.* London: Macmillan and Company, Ltd., 1917–18. (pp. 398–399)

     . . . children lose their teeth. . . . Frazer, *The Golden Bough, Part I, The Magic Art and the Evolution of Kings,* vol. 1. (p. 178)

p. 50   Frazer, *The Golden Bough, Part V, Spirits of the Corn and of the Wild*, vol. 2. (p. 281)

pp. 50 & 51   *Four pairs of mice.* . . . Ibid., (p. 278)

p. 54   1 Sam. 5:12

pp. 55 & 56   Barbanson, Adrienne. *Fables in Ivory*. Vermont: Charles E. Tuttle Co., 1961. (pp. 42 and 82)

pp. 56–58   *The index read.* . . . Teale, Edwin Way. *North with the Spring*. New York: Dodd, Mead & Co., 1951.

pp. 61 & 62   Krutch, Joseph Wood. *The World of Animals*. New York: Simon & Schuster, 1961. (p. 309)

pp. 72 & 73   Durrell, Gerald. *The Bafut Beagles*. New York: The Viking Press, 1954. (pp. 208–210)

pp. 82 & 83   Carrighar, Sally. *Wild Heritage*. Boston: Houghton Mifflin Co., 1965. (p. 228)

p. 84   Opie, Iona and Peter. *A Family Book of Nursery Rhymes*. New York: Oxford University Press, 1964. (pp. 84–85)

pp. 85–87   Sanderson, Ivan T. *Living Mammals of the World*. New York: Doubleday, 1955. (pp. 114–155)

p. 87   *"pallid wraith of a beach mouse."* Barbour, Thomas. *That Vanishing Eden: A Naturalist's Florida*. Boston: Little, Brown and Company, 1944. (p. 194)

pp. 88 & 89   Koenig, Lilli. *Nature Stories from the Vienna Woods*. Translated by Marjorie Latzke. New York: Thomas Y. Crowell Co., 1959.

p. 94   Dyson, Robert H. "Art of the Twin Rivers." *Natural History*, June-July, 1962.

pp. 95–98   Terres, John K. "Search for the Golden Mouse." *Audubon Magazine*, March-April, 1966.

Books the Doolan Family Used

p. 100   Peterson, Willis. "Meet Dipo." *Audubon Magazine*, March-
             April, 1968.

pp. 110–111 Desroches-Noblecourt, Christaine. *Egyptian Wall Paintings:
             From Tombs and Temples.* The New York American
             Library of World Literature, 1962. A Mentor UNESCO
             Art Book. (Plate 12)

             Editors of Horizon Magazine. *The Horizon Book of Lost
             Worlds.* Narrative by Leonard Cottrell. New York:
             (American Heritage) Doubleday, 1962.

             Sanderson, *Living Mammals of the World.* (pp. 145–146)

BOOK ONE

Sir Arthur Conan Doyle's

THE ADVENTURES OF SHERLOCK HOLMES

Adapted for young readers by Catherine Edwards Sadler

Whose footsteps are those on the stairs of 221-B Baker Street, home of Mr. Sherlock Holmes, the world's greatest detective? And what incredible mysteries will challenge the wits of the genius sleuth this time?

A Study In Scarlet In the first Sherlock Holmes story ever written, Holmes and Watson embark on their first case together—an intriguing murder mystery.

The Red-headed League Holmes comes to the rescue in a most unusual heist!

The Man With The Twisted Lip Is this a case of murder, kidnapping, or something totally unexpected?

Join the uncanny and extraordinary Sherlock Holmes, and his friend and chronicler, Dr. Watson as they tackle dangerous crimes and untangle the most intricate mysteries.

AVON CAMELOT

AN AVON CAMELOT ORIGINAL • 78089 • $1.95
(ISBN: 0-380-78089-5)

Avon Camelot Books are available at your bookstore. Or, you may use Avon's special mail order service. Please state the title and code number and send with your check or money order for the full price, plus 50¢ per copy to cover postage and handling, to: AVON BOOKS, Mail Order Department, 224 West 57th Street, New York, New York 10019.

Please allow 6-8 weeks for delivery.